Christopher Quirk
Illustrations by Eleonora Cali

The Day the Colours Went Away

Bumblebee Books
London

A CIP catalogue record for this title is
available from the British Library.

ISBN: 978-1-83934-332-2

Bumblebee Books is an imprint of
Olympia Publishers.

First Published in 2021

Bumblebee Books
Tallis House
2 Tallis Street
London
EC4Y 0AB

Printed in Great Britain

www.olympiapublishers.com

Dedication

To my wife, Lisa, thank you for keeping the ship steady to enable the dream to continue. Without your unquestionable devotion to our children nothing would be possible.

A little mouse woke up
In the dark in his bed.
No light to turn on
The colour was dead,
The windows were pale,
The walls and the floors,
The ceiling was blank
And so were the doors.

There were clouds in the sky
But no golden sun.
No red morning light,
No colours to run,
No green on the grass,
No orange in the trees,
There was nothing but grey
And a cold windy breeze.

No crisp purple sheets
Reflecting the suns rays,
He fell out of bed
Half in a daze.
Stumbled downstairs
And out of his door,
Nothing quite seemed
Like it was before.

Then he ventured out
Into the street,
He checked just to see
If the world was complete,
But everyone around
Was exactly the same.
No difference at all, and
No one they could blame.

The confusion was real,
The little mouse couldn't accept
Where had the colour gone
Whilst everyone had slept.
Everything was calm
No emotion in the air,
No anger or hate,
No protests for the unfair.

He walked down the road
And then kept on going.
Over the river
Which was still flowing,
Towards the pond
And over the log.
He finally stopped
When he noticed a frog.

What's going on?
The frog just jumped by
But the mouse could not tell
If he caught his eye.
"Is he like me?
Can't he see it too?
It's all just the same,
No yellow, red or blue."

Another mouse ran over,
He lived on his street,
He worked at the cheese factory,
He seemed very upbeat.
"How are you?" he said.
"Isn't this mad,
We all look the same.
I don't think its that bad."

"We are both equal,
I must declare,
Your grey face
And your grey hair.
Your voice, its tone,
Your eyes and their shine,
Everything about you
Is the same as mine."

The plucky mouse was right
You can't tell them apart.
Every mouse and their child,
It's like a fresh start.
They learn the same things,
They grow the same way,
They make different choices,
They get old one day.

The clouds began to part
And some light returned.
Slowly at first
Then like fire, it burned.
It ripped through the sky
And tore through the land.
It was powerful and strong,
It was great and was grand.

The light kept going
Until every colour was back.
Perfect and vibrant,
No sign of a crack.
And yet something had changed
That would not be forgot,
The colours have returned
But their meanings did not.

For what was there
Had always been so
It just took a moment
For the colour to go.
To realise the truth
And one simple fact
That the difference in colour
Should never come back.

About the Author

Prolific children's book writer, Christopher Quirk, began his writing career as a hobby. He wrote short stories and poems in his spare time as a head space and mind clearing exercise. Teaming with multiple illustrators he has now bought these stories to life for your enjoyment. He lives in the UK in Essex and his new mission is to publish books that his young daughter and son will enjoy and cherish. The byproduct of this is the books commercially available today. He regularly posts reviews, previews of new books, and lots of fun stuff on his Instagram page @thealexanderbooks.

Other books available by Christopher Quirk

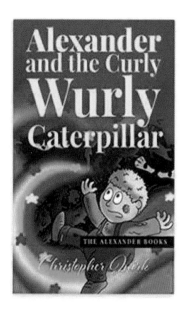

Alexander and the Curly
Wurly Caterpillar (The
Alexander Books): 1

Annabelle and the Talking
Squawking Ducks (The
Alexander Books): 2

My Grandma Lives In A
Treehouse

Printed in Great Britain
by Amazon